# AGENT 355

# AGENT 355

## *A Novella*

## Marie Benedict

OPEN ROAD
INTEGRATED MEDIA
NEW YORK

ISBN: 978-1-5040-9095-7

This edition published in 2024 by Open Road Integrated Media, Inc.
180 Maiden Lane
New York, NY 10038
www.openroadmedia.com

# AGENT 355

# CHAPTER 1

September 28, 1779
New York, New York

The staccato clip sounds like gunfire. I flinch with each sound, but it's only my mother's heels reverberating on the polished wooden floor of the hallway, and I know exactly what she seeks. Me.

"Elizabeth," she calls to me while pushing open the door to the library, my haven. "I cannot believe you're still in your day gown. Why aren't you dressed for the DeLanceys' party? Your father and I are waiting for you in the front hallway."

"Mother, I've already told you that I'd prefer not to attend." I gesture to the copy of John Locke's *Two Treatises of Government* I've been reading by candlelight. While I don't agree with all of Locke's views, I certainly concur with his argument that the only legitimate governments are those that govern with their people's consent. I particularly like his notion that patriarchalism approved by God does not exist. Not that my mother would care to hear my perspective. "Locke is company enough," I say.

She glances behind her, to the front door of our house. I know she is ensuring that no one is within earshot—or eyeshot.

"Put that away, Elizabeth. You cannot be seen reading John Locke. That text is practically heresy since the instigators of the Revolution cited it. I should never have let you visit your Aunt Floyd in Connecticut, filling your head with that nonsense about freedom and giving you unfettered access to my father's old library. The ideas in that book will get you thrown on a British prison ship."

She *tsks* at me, shaking her head. "Anyway, you must attend the party because we must keep up appearances. Now more than ever."

"I doubt that anyone at the DeLanceys' will notice whether your eighteen-year-old, bookish daughter is in attendance or not, Mother."

She draws very close to me, the skirt of her maroon China-silk gown swishing along the floor. Lowering her voice to a sharp whisper, almost a hiss, she says, "Do you think that the officer quartering with us will be oblivious to your absence? Do you think that Officer Randolph won't take note that you've chosen to stay home instead of celebrating the arrival of General Clinton and Major André into the city? You don't have the luxury of refusing. None of us does. Not anymore."

Knowing she will brook no more resistance, I hasten to my room and choose the buttercup-yellow silk gown embroidered with cornflower-blue vines and floral sprigs. It has a square bodice and a beaded, triangular stomacher that overlays a skirt of matching blue. Our maid, Susan, helps me into it and then sweeps my dark-blonde hair into a formal style before pinching some color into my cheeks. My parents greet me with silent disdain when I finally join them. Neither approves of lateness, even in less trying times.

Custom would typically require we travel by carriage to the party, but the DeLanceys live only one short block from our home near Bowling Green and the governor's mansion, and my parents have determined to walk. We step outside, and I immediately wonder how they can bear this heat. Until recently, I've spent my summers at my mother's family estate in rural Connecticut, now run by her brother's widow, Evangeline Floyd, and her young sons. I was spared the wilting warmth and pungent smells of city summers. Family and friends alike are quick to mention that this summer is unusually warm and particularly foul because of the rise in population as Loyalist refugees continue to flood the British-protected city from nearby areas falling to the Continental Army. But I doubt this summer is very unique.

The moon is nearly full, casting enough light on the road that my mother and I can tread carefully. The British preserved this genteel section of the city throughout their battle so that they could enjoy it during their occupation, but even so, the cobblestones lining the street are uneven, and garbage litters the streets. I try to allow the noises of the city to distract me from the heaviness of my mood, but the sounds of carriage wheels on stone and horses' whinnies do nothing to lighten the weight upon me.

My parents have never held any particularly strong political convictions—aligning themselves instead with whatever faction held control and supported my father's import business—and so compulsory attendance at this social occasion honoring the British does not trouble them. But the sight of Redcoats amidst our friends, raising a glass to celebrate these times, enrages me. Have people obliterated from their memories the list of abuses the British heaped upon the colonies in the years leading up to the Revolution? Even more important, how can people forget the storming of New York, the retreat of General Washington and his Continental Army, the killing of so many New Yorkers, and the imprisoning of even more in the dreaded prison ships my mother just threatened? My mother blames my Aunt Floyd for my views. I confess to learning about the ideology of the Continental Congress through conversations with her and the books at her home, but I have arrived at my distrust of the British and their motives from what I've observed firsthand: their greed and arrogance as they help themselves to our homes and our land and our money through endless rounds of taxes and quartering, without offering even minimal representation in return.

The sound of violins and flutes grows louder, drowning out the noise of carriages as we near the DeLanceys' house. It is similar to ours with its yellow Holland-brick exterior, three stories, and columned entry. My father turns toward us with a smile and says—in a rare, though oblique, acknowledgement—that war is in our midst. "It sounds lovely. My family deserves a bit of merriment after much turmoil."

Laughter streams out the open windows along with the music, and I gather my skirts to climb the three steps to the front door of the house. Mr. and Mrs. DeLancey greet us in the entryway with warm embraces for me and my mother and a hearty handshake for my father. They direct us into the drawing room, presided over by the requisite John Singleton Copley family portrait, of course. Every good family seems to have one, for not only is he talented, but his wife comes from a family of well-known, staunch Crown supporters. We continue into the parlor, where the dancing has already begun.

The shock of red from the British officers' uniforms disrupts the scene, drawing the eye away from the gentle flow of the dancers and the soft colors of their blue, yellow, brown, and green attire. The officer stationed with us, Officer Randolph, nods in our direction but doesn't break away for a proper welcome. He's too busy holding court with his newly arrived superiors, British Commander-in-Chief Gen. Henry Clinton and his Adjutant Gen. Maj. John André. After returning the nod of recognition, my parents enter the fold of revelers, but such a seamless entrée isn't so simple for me. Not only have I never felt fully at ease with the women of my acquaintance, but I cannot mingle with the men with the same flirtatious ease. It's one thing to greet the British at church on Sunday or to pass them at the high street, but to drink and eat and dance alongside them feels wrong. I must be careful not to let my sentiments show.

I walk to the dining room, where a sumptuous repast of ham, lamb, herbed potatoes, fresh bread, and a bounty of fruits and vegetables is spread upon the table next to Wedgwood china plates, silver implements, and crystal goblets. How did the DeLanceys manage this abundance of food? The British occupy most of Long Island and all of New York City—a blow to General Washington's strategy of keeping these key geographic and financial regions in his control—and getting food into the city from the farms in the surrounding countryside is no easy feat. Battlefields are often crossed in order to feed New Yorkers.

I linger at the edge of the table, idly picking at a small plate of ham and potatoes and hoping I appear occupied enough to avoid an invitation to dance. Although, given the relative paucity of men compared to women, I suppose I should not worry. The DeLanceys' party has girls aplenty—and they're not only willing but excited to dance with the British soldiers. The arrival of the British into New York has resulted not only in martial law, but in the occupiers' unquenchable thirst for gaiety, yielding an unprecedented whirl of parties, musical recitals, balls, plays, card tournaments, and weekends of fox-hunting, cricket, horse racing, and golf, the likes of which have never been seen before.

With all this forced merriment, it can be hard to remember that we are a nation at war.

My back stiffens as a small cadre of officers enters the dining room, but I relax when they gather around the corner of the table farthest from me. They've come here to talk, not to find dance partners. So as not to draw any sort of attention to myself, I lean against the china cabinet with the chinoiserie fretwork and feign complete interest in my food, pushing it around on my plate with a fork. But in truth, I need not bother. I am invisible to these men. I know they don't believe me capable of understanding their military conversations, and they presume my disinterest.

"With Major André here in New York, we're certain to round up those damn traitors hiding in Connecticut and New Jersey and lay waste to their damned uprising in no time," one of the officers mutters to the two others.

The darker-haired officer nods. "He'll find a way to get his hands on Washington's plans and rout those bastards before they can do further damage."

"I hear that André has already assembled a team of spies to ferret out Washington's schemes," the first officer says. The men chortle, probably already envisioning their victory over the despised general.

So Major André is in New York City as a spymaster, not as adjutant general to British Commander-in-Chief General Clinton, as has been publicly claimed. *Interesting.* I have always loathed the way men have dismissed me in matters of government and intellect, but now I wonder whether it might be an asset. What else might an invisible woman be able to learn?

# CHAPTER 2

My solitude, with its fortuitous eavesdropping, does not last long. Old family friends, Mr. and Mrs. Llewellyn, approach me with a burly British officer at their side.

"Miss Morris, how delightful to see you so early in the season! You usually don't return to the city until October," Mrs. Llewellyn exclaims.

"An unusual time calls for unusual measures," I answer with muted frankness. "My visit to my mother's family farm was very brief this year, as it was the year before."

Mr. and Mrs. Llewellyn glance at each other, considering my roundabout reference to the war. Direct conversation about the military situation by or with an unmarried woman is considered unsuitable—no matter that the female family members of Continental Army soldiers are directly involved in the war, particularly in Philadelphia, through their formation of a Ladies Association to raise money for their effort. I can see them weighing how best to respond.

"It lies precariously close to rebel territory, from what I understand," Mr. Llewellyn comments. "Better to have you here in the city, where you are safely surrounded by the British military."

Mrs. Llewellyn redirects the discussion to an always appropriate topic: "Well, it certainly has been a strangely hot September."

"That's what I've been told."

We continue exchanging pleasantries about the weather and the music until Mr. Llewellyn clears his throat and gestures to the officer to his left. "Miss Morris, we'd like to introduce you to Colonel Moss. We have the honor of hosting him while he's in New York."

Most families of our acquaintance have the "honor" of having one of the higher-ranking British officers board with them, though quartering is not an honor they can safely refuse.

I give Colonel Moss a half curtsy, while he offers a greeting. "It's a pleasure to meet you, Miss Morris."

In the quiet that overcomes the Llewellyns, I surmise what Colonel Moss is working toward—a request to dance. When he finally stammers out his invitation, I shiver at the thought of being wrapped in those blood-red arms and having them direct me around the dance floor, but protocol won't permit me to decline. So I accept.

We make our way to the marble dance floor. When the musicians strike their opening chord, I'm relieved to hear that they're not playing a minuet. That traditional dance requires one couple to dance at a time, which means the rest of the partygoers watch. The very notion is excruciating. Instead, the trio of musicians plays an allemande, and the dancers assemble into two lines, women on one side and men on the other. We take turns pairing with our partner and dancing a particular step between the two lines, then wait while the others do the same. I watch the movements of other couples, noting that everyone seems to be enjoying this but me. The unmarried young ladies relish the attention lavished upon them by the British officers who've taken up residence in our city, and prefer their gleaming uniforms and the pomp of their manner to the less formal demeanor and ragtag appearance of the Continental Army. Time and time again, I'm reminded that women, we young ladies in particular, are meant to have the same opinions as the heads of our households. I cannot imagine relinquishing my ideas and reaching a place of acceptance like my father has.

The song mercifully comes to an end, and I'm about to take my leave from Colonel Moss when the musicians begin a hornpipe dance. The colonel keeps ahold of my hand and launches into the freeform dance, spinning me into another couple with such force that I feel the need to apologize for the collision. He seems not to notice and continues with his fervent dancing. I spot my mother on the periphery of the dance floor lined with Chippendale cabinets and presided over by a tall walnut case clock and I give her a beseeching look, unsure what help she can offer but feeling desperate. Rather than finding some appropriate way to extricate me, she gives me a broad grin, a certain signal that she would like a smile in return. To appease her, and to spare myself the upbraiding I would otherwise receive at home, I give her a half smile, which Colonel Moss mistakenly believes is directed at him.

His fingers clutch me tighter as the pace of the hornpipe dance quickens. We brush up against fellow couples, who are also whirling around the compact space. Finally, the music slows as the dance ends, but instead of being released from the colonel's arms, I find myself being steered backward, off the dance floor and into a dark, empty corridor leading to the kitchen. This nook is out of sight of the dance floor.

"It's nice to meet a welcoming girl from the colonies. Many of your women are rather prim, to say the least," he says, pulling me closer to him.

"I'm not certain what you mean," I answer, craning my face and neck away from him.

"How coy you are," he says with a leer. "I bring you close, and you pretend to pull away."

"I-I think you've misunderstood—" I back away as best I can, given that his arms are around my waist in a vise-like grip.

He interrupts me. "It seems that we are doing the push-pull dance of the colonies. A losing dance for those that resist, of course."

"I think I'd prefer to be liberated, sir," I answer, trying desperately to extricate myself from his hold.

He squeezes me to him, an audacious maneuver. Why isn't anyone intervening? Is it possible that no one can see us? Or have they all turned a blind eye to this brute's behavior because he's a British officer?

His voice hardens, as does his expression. "Are you saying that you—you're a rebel? That you'd like to *liberate* the colonies from the Crown?"

Dismay turns to fear at his transformation, and I protest, "No, no, that's not what I meant. Not at all. I merely meant that I'd like to be liberated from *dancing*."

Bringing his face close enough to mine that I can smell the wine on his breath, he says, "I don't think that's your only meaning."

Equal measures of terror and fury rise up within me and threaten to erupt when suddenly a hand appears on the soldier's shoulder. Colonel Moss's face reddens in anger, and when he turns to face the trespasser, he loosens his grip on my waist. As I stumble backward from the release of his hold, I hear a voice say, "I think she's had quite enough dancing, sir."

# CHAPTER 3

"Are you all right?" a deep voice asks me after the colonel has taken his leave. Not without a fair bit of shoving and protestations.

"I am, sir," I answer in as steady a voice as I can muster, as we move away from the dark corner of the hallway toward a brighter area with a view of the dance floor. Smoothing my skirt, I square my shoulders and assume my full height, average though that may be. "I'm grateful to you for your aid."

"It's what any man would do in the situation," my rescuer answers. I take a moment to study him. Tall and lanky, he has a long nose balanced by high cheekbones and a strong jaw, with soft brown eyes. But the most striking thing about him is the fact that he's strangely underdressed for the occasion. While the other male guests are dressed in uniform, or wear waistcoats under long jackets so heavily embroidered that they resemble the women's gowns, this gentleman wears simple black linen breeches and an unadorned jacket of tan cotton.

I gesture down the long hallway to the room where dancing continues, unabated. "I beg to differ."

He shrugs, as if his intervention was nothing. But then his eyes narrow and his voice vibrates with anger, belying the nonchalance of his gesture. "I couldn't allow a young lady to suffer at the hands of a brute, no matter what uniform he wears."

"The uniform does seem to have emboldened him." I pause, still shaken and angry at the soldier's rough and presumptuous behavior, and I blurt out the belief I've long held but kept silent. "The British think they can take whatever they wish, even when it doesn't belong to them. They overstep their bounds and abuse their power."

Luckily, his tone softens, becoming compassionate. "My sister suffered similarly at the hands of a British solider, miss, and so I have an uncommon familiarity with your situation and, possibly, your feelings."

My hand flies to my mouth. "Is your sister all right, sir?"

"Yes, fortunately. The lieutenant colonel who quarters with my family in Long Island made unwanted advances, but now that my father is aware, he has ensured that my sister is protected at all times. Of course, he would prefer that this officer not remain in his home, particularly after he destroyed the orchards and relegated the family to a few back rooms, but as I'm sure you know, any sort of objection is subject to punishment or—if the resistance is deemed traitorous—death."

"I know all too well," I reply, glancing at the British officer we have been forced to board. "I cannot thank you enough for your assistance, Mister . . ." I hesitate, as the gentleman never mentioned his name.

"My apologies, miss. In the circumstances, I didn't have the chance to introduce myself. My name is Robert Townsend, and I am at your service," he says with a brief bow in my direction.

"I am Elizabeth Morris, and it's a pleasure to make your acquaintance." I bob down in a half curtsy, wondering why his name sounds familiar. "Are you in the city from Long Island only for the evening, Mr. Townsend?" Perhaps an unexpected trip to the city from the countryside explains his casual attire.

"No, Miss Morris, I've made the city my home for some time. My father apprenticed me to the merchant house Templeton & Stewart in New York City when I was in my teens. I stayed until about two years ago. I loathed working in the district near the docks. It was good for business, but not for the soul."

He doesn't need to elaborate further. The area near the docks, on Barclay, Church, and Vesey Streets, services the needs of incoming ships, whose sailors require goods and services, the latter being of a . . . less savory sort.

He continues, "At that time, I started my own concern, a dry goods shop close to the Fly Market on Maiden Lane." I recognize the name—our cook visits there regularly.

"How wonderful to have your own business, free from the involvement of others. But don't you miss the family farm?" I ask, a bit wistful for my own summers in Connecticut.

"Well, I miss my family, but I never was much of a farmer."

"Really? I miss being out in the fields and the freshness of the rural landscape. Most years, I live with my parents in the city only from autumn through spring. Until the war took hold of New York, I was fortunate enough to spend every summer at my mother's family farm in Connecticut, ever since I was a small child. That all changed, though."

"I would ask why, but I think I can guess at the answer."

"I'm certain you can. My parents didn't want me to stay in a region with so much support for the Continental Army. It could hurt my father's business for their daughter to be seen living among rebels—as they put it—and they insisted I return to the city. As you know, a merchant's success rises and falls with the British these days." I pause before continuing, wondering how much more I can say aloud to this Mr. Townsend, even though he seems sympathetic to my views. But I dare to speak my mind. "I miss the freedom of the Connecticut countryside. In more ways than one."

He lowers his voice. "I appreciate your candor, Miss Morris, and I echo your perspective. But I urge you to be judicious in sharing your opinions here."

I glance down at the floor, momentarily embarrassed. *How foolish*, I think. *This man could be anyone, even a British spy.* "You're the only person with whom I've shared them," I answer honestly. Well, mostly honestly, as I do converse with Aunt Floyd on the topic of the British.

"And I'm honored. But after tonight's encounter, I feel unusually protective of you."

"I appreciate your chivalry, Mr. Townsend." To bring the conversation onto safer ground, as he has requested, I ask a more innocuous question. "From where on Long Island does your family hail?"

"Their farm is near Oyster Bay, as is their shop and fleet of trading ships. My family resides on the property."

"Ah, that's why the Townsend name is familiar! Distant cousins of mine, the Floyds, live on Long Island—not too far from Oyster Bay. Or least they *did*, until the British confiscated their home and they were forced to flee to Connecticut. Are you familiar with William Floyd and his family?"

He nods in recognition, but drops his already low voice to a whisper to reply. "I am indeed. Although I don't know that mentioning his name here will make you very popular. William Floyd is a signer of the Declaration of Independence, and he fought against the British when they first attacked Long Island."

"I know," I whisper back with a smile. "I'll keep your secret if you keep mine."

"What do you mean?" he asks, his eyebrows arching.

"Your father is Samuel Townsend, if I'm not mistaken?"

"You are correct, Miss." His voice is wary.

"I've heard stories about Samuel Townsend of Oyster Bay, and I understand he has a history of disagreements with the Crown's policies."

"So you do know my family." He nods reluctantly. "My father's willingness to challenge the British when he believes they've abused their power is one reason why the detestable Lieutenant Colonel Simcoe I mentioned decided to take up residence in our family home along with his troops. It was a form of punishment, I believe, even after my father reversed his position and took an oath to support the Crown."

"I'm sorry to hear that, Mr. Townsend." I give him a half smile. "But it does seem as though you are following in your father's footsteps."

"I did have a good teacher." He smiles back at me, a subdued grin that I suspect he bestows only rarely, and never falsely. Then he says, "Well, Miss Morris, it seems we're in accord. Of course, I agree to your request to keep each other's secrets." For a long moment, we share that grin, having made this unexpected connection.

But then, a thought penetrates this pleasing synchronicity. What is this gentleman doing at this Loyalist gathering? In his dress and in his views, he seems the most unlikely of guests. I, at least, have reasons for my attendance—my gender and the insistence of my parents.

I ask, "What brings you to the DeLanceys tonight? Are you friends with our hosts?"

"No. I'm actually here in my capacity as a writer for the *Royal Gazette*. I occasionally cover social occasions if they're particularly newsworthy, and since this event honors the newly arrived Major André and General Clinton, it's of interest."

*How peculiar,* I think, *is this occupation for a man of his temperament and beliefs, particularly since he's undoubtedly busy running his own establishment.* But I don't say so. Instead, I say, "Oh, my. I've been very frank with no less than a writer for a Loyalist newspaper. You're a man who wears many hats."

"I find it keeps my body busy and my mind occupied in these troubling times," he says, without addressing the incongruity between his views and his work.

"I wish I could do the same. We women are constricted to our limited cycle of activities and our small sphere, especially here in the city. A broader view prevails in the countryside."

"Not always. It's much the same for my sisters, even though they live on a farm," he says.

In the corner of my vision, I see my mother gesturing to me. I'm reluctant to leave this unusual man, but I know my mother will tolerate only a modicum of independence. "I must take my leave, Mr. Townsend, but I thank you. And I hope our paths cross again." While these words constitute a common enough farewell, I mean them most sincerely. I have some ideas about exactly why Mr. Townsend is in attendance tonight. And after experiencing the British mistreatment firsthand tonight, I can be complacent no more.

# CHAPTER 4

October 14, 1779
New York, New York

"How agreeable you've become lately, Elizabeth." The pleasure in my mother's voice is obvious.

After the DeLanceys' party, I decided to become fully immersed in my mother's world for the first time in my life. I began to join her in her daily circle of activities—from mornings overseeing our three servants and the cook, the menu, and the household's laundry and cleaning schedule; to afternoons making social calls to our neighbors, attending services at church, and taking walks in Bowling Green; to evenings attending dinners and parties or undertaking needlework projects. The sameness of her days, with the lack of time alone in restorative solitude, simultaneously numbs and exhausts me. But I have a plan.

"I've been resistant for far too long, Mother," I answer, and she squeezes my hand in delight. I feel guilty feigning interest in the activities of my mother's realm, but there is no other way.

"It's good to see you interested in acquiring the skills necessary to please a husband." She smiles. "Perhaps we'll see you work on modesty and delicacy next."

On a typical day, the errand at hand wouldn't have merited my mother's personal attention. She would have left the pick of meats and fishes to Cook, merely approving them—or not—when they arrived in the kitchen. But tonight, we are hosting a dinner for several friends and their quartering officers, and she insists on making the selection herself at the market. A successful event is key to my father's business.

The vestiges of summer heat have finally left, and the day is refreshingly crisp and bright, so we decide to walk to the market. The city reverberates with the sound of hammers on wood and axes on stone, as the workers rebuild the houses and shops that were destroyed by fire from the fighting some time ago. The British blamed the Continental Army for the destruction, of course, but the damage could just as easily have emanated from a rogue cannon blast on the part of the British. Either way, with the surging Loyalist population, the city needs the additional housing that this new construction will provide.

Passing countless people with red badges on their hats as a token of their loyalty to the Crown, I trail after my mother down Maiden Lane until it ends at Front Street, facing the East River. There, we enter the Fly Market, where the city's best produce, fish, and meat are sold by vendors under a covered roof. As my mother studies the offerings at the various stalls, I try to catch a glimpse of the shops bordering the market, and I finally spot it: Townsend's Dry Goods Shop.

"Mother," I say as she compares the cuts of meat at a favored vendor, "do you mind if I stop into a store we passed for some needlework supplies? I'll return here right away."

She waves at me, distracted. "Yes, but don't tarry."

I weave through the bustling market to the store I spied, hoping I'll have enough time to carry out my plan before

Mother seeks me out. It's only as I approach Mr. Townsend's store that I wonder for the first time whether my proposal will be well received. I have been musing on it for the last few weeks, so fixated on the means by which I could access Mr. Townsend's store that I haven't even thought of what he might say.

Nerves set in as I push open the door to the shop, especially when I see the back of a worker behind the counter, tending to the needs of a few older women. What if Mr. Townsend isn't even at the shop today? I hadn't thought through that possibility, either.

I wait as the merchant fetches a burlap sack of flour and hands it to his customer. Then he finally faces me, and I realize it's Mr. Townsend himself.

"Miss Morris," he says when he notices me, an arched eyebrow the only evidence of his surprise.

"I've come for some supplies, Mr. Townsend. I'll be happy for your assistance once you've finished with your customers."

He keeps his eyes on me as he completes the transactions and, one by one, the women leave the shop. When the door slams shut on the final customer, he turns to me, saying, "What a surprise, Miss Morris. I'm pleased to see you, of course, but I never expected we would encounter one another here. I thought I'd have to wait until I was covering another social occasion for the *Royal Gazette*."

"Why should I not see you while I attend to errands in Fly Market? I accompany my mother as she undertakes her housewifely duties."

"You don't strike me as the sort of woman who relishes those errands . . ."

While a continuation of this exchange of pleasantries would typically be required, I don't have the time. At any moment, my mother could finish her shopping and hunt me down.

Squaring my shoulders, I come to the point in a hushed tone. "I visit you today because I feel certain we share the same views about the British occupation of New York. And elsewhere in the colonies."

"You are correct in that assumption," he answers warily.

"Good. I'll get right to it then: I would like to serve the Revolution. I am so tired of watching as the British destroy our land and harm our citizens. I believe in the cause of freedom."

"I appreciate your sentiments, but . . . how could you be of use?"

"Simply because I'm a young woman living an affluent life doesn't mean that I'm without my own independent views, or without *use*. Surely a man of your background and proclivities understands that."

He pauses, then says, "Fair enough. But I'm not certain why you think *I* might be the person to put your services to good purpose."

"Well, you are a man with a demanding business to run, yet you have elected to spend your rare hours outside the shop writing articles for a Loyalist newspaper. All this despite the fact that you support the Revolution, your own family has espoused views against the Crown, and your family's property has been subjected to destruction by the British occupying it. I can think of only one reason you would choose to spend your spare time writing for the *Royal Gazette*."

"And what is that reason?" he asks, his posture rigid.

"Gathering information that might be helpful to the Continental Army," I whisper.

Without directly responding to my supposition, he asks another question. "You do realize that having views that are aligned with the Revolution, and actually being of value to it, are two entirely different things?"

"Mr. Townsend, I believe that I could serve in a uniquely valuable capacity and deliver information to you—that no one else can assemble."

"How so?"

Here, I know just how to prove my value. "You are familiar with Major André?"

"Of course," he says, the surprise evident in his voice. "Officially, he's General Clinton's aide, but I'm sure you know there's suspicion that he's actually an intelligence officer. But why do you ask?"

"Have you ever actually spoken to the man?"

Mr. Townsend stares at me for a long moment, then concedes, "No. How could I possibly get access to a British officer of that rank? Even while acting on behalf of the *Royal Gazette*, I'm limited to asking questions of the host and hostess of these events, and making observations."

"Well, I've conversed with him on several occasions, and observed him on many more. There are things I can report already: he is artistic, a favorite with the ladies, and hails from a monied background in Switzerland and England. Once he inherited some wealth for himself, he bought himself a position with the Fusiliers, but transferred to the Seventh Foot, heading to Quebec. He then became a staff officer and translator for General Howe, as his family background afforded him the opportunity to learn several languages. When Howe left, he joined General Clinton's staff, and that's when he began to experience real success. His friendship with Clinton led to his rise from simple subaltern to adjutant general, but that title is in name only—I can confirm that he serves primarily as the chief spy for the British."

By the time I finish, Mr. Townsend's mouth is agape. "How do you know all that?"

"By listening to conversations that no one thinks I'm able to comprehend. The British, like all men, speak freely in front of women. Invisibility has its benefits."

He grows quiet, this already quiet man. Finally, he speaks. "You are an unusual young lady."

"And these are unusual times." I meet his gaze and ask, "Do you accept my offer?"

Mr. Townsend, the essence of solemnity, lets out an unexpected laugh. "I don't think I could forestall your efforts, even if I declined. So, yes, Miss Morris, I accept."

# CHAPTER 5

November 23, 1779
New York, New York

I can barely wait until our next market day. On Tuesdays and Thursdays, our cook walks to Fly Market to procure supplies, and I've made it a habit to accompany her. Mother was quizzical at first, but when I attributed it to my burgeoning interest in helpmate skills, she seemed pleased. And thank goodness for that, because about six weeks after Mr. Townsend and I agreed to work together, I finally have a real story to report.

What if the British should put their plan into motion before I have the opportunity to share the details? This thought plagues me as the hours pass with molasses-like slowness from Saturday to Sunday to Monday, but I have no way of getting to the market without Cook or Mother and an adequate excuse. An unmarried young lady simply does not venture out into the city without an approved purpose or a chaperone.

When Tuesday finally arrives, I insist that Cook and I set out for the market as soon as breakfast finishes. We head out to the busy city streets at Cook's frustratingly slow pace, passing by buildings pockmarked from bullets, and I think about how

Mr. Townsend will respond to my new information. To me, the overheard scheme seems critical, but will he be pleased? Is it significant enough to act upon? Reliable enough? I wonder why his reaction means so much to me, why I am moved to gratify this quiet, serious man.

As I had with Mother, I pretend to be interested in the comparisons of produce and meats at the different stalls, then take my leave under the pretense of needing needlework supplies. Checking behind me to ensure Cook is fully engaged in her interrogation of a merchant, I head to Townsend's Dry Goods Shop.

The door slams shut with a loud thud behind me, startling Mr. Townsend, who sits behind the counter with a ledger. "Miss Morris, you came," he says, as if he thought I'd never return. As if I haven't visited his store every Tuesday and Thursday since our meeting, each time bringing some new, albeit small, nugget of information.

"Of course I did. And I bear gifts. Is now a good time?" I glance around the store.

"It is. We are alone." His somber countenance brightens as a warm smile overtakes it.

"Very good. I dined at the home of Mr. and Mrs. Van Cortlandt on Saturday evening where Major André was in attendance." I pause, assessing his reaction. I notice that he's leaned forward slightly, in expectation. "In order to get close to André, I accepted a dance with one of his men, and after it concluded, we joined the major and three other officers for a refreshment, including that terrible Colonel Moss. The usual conversation about music and dancing ensued, and then I stepped aside to speak with a neighbor in close proximity to the men."

"Did you overhear anything?"

"I did. At first, they exchanged a few unpleasant words about the Continental Army, stating that the 'rebels,' as they call them, mistakenly believe that securing Philadelphia is the key to winning the war, because the Continental Congress is located there. The men laughed at this, reinforcing the point that New York is the key to victory. I despaired initially, thinking they would all agree, giving reasons why New York is so important and patting one another on the back for their success."

I take a deep breath before continuing. "But then the conversation changed, as did the men's tone. Major André said, 'If only the rebels knew *why* Philadelphia has proven to be so important. And helpful.' The men laughed, and then the awful Colonel Moss said, 'Have they learned that we've procured several reams of their precious currency paper from Philadelphia?' André responded that there had been nothing to indicate any such awareness, and that, in fact, the government was proceeding with its usual printing—as he put it—its 'blasted Continentals.'"

Mr. Townsend is immobile, as if the words are too potent to process. But I have to proceed—we only have so much time alone. "An officer I don't know asked, 'Have we received the paper and the plates yet?' André responded that the items were en route and due to arrive in New York City within a couple of days. Then he said, 'We can print our own Continentals and flood the market with them until the damned dollars are value-less.' To which Moss replied, 'While our own sterling currency only rises.'"

"My god," Mr. Townsend whispers, but when he doesn't add more, I continue.

"I think it's clear that the British have stolen the neces-sary materials to embark on a plan to produce counterfeit Continental money, a scheme that will devalue the dollar and make it almost impossible for General Washington to get the necessary supplies to win the war." I pause for a brief moment, waiting for his concurrence. When he still doesn't respond, I ask, "Don't you agree, Mr. Townsend?"

He looks at me, but still doesn't speak. Finally rousing himself, Mr. Townsend nods. "You are certain about what André and the other men said?"

"Absolutely."

"Then they must have breached the safeguard the government placed upon our currency to protect it from this exact scenario." Despite the seriousness of the situation, he manages a smile for me. "This is excellent work, Miss Morris. We have the chance to stop this scheme in its tracks. I cannot thank you enough for this."

"I am delighted to be of service." I smile back at him. "I told you my invisibility might prove useful."

He nods, then stoops down behind the counter and begins rifling through objects on a low shelf and says, "I will need to get word of this plan out immediately. Before it's too late."

I follow him as he moves about the shop, gathering paper and pulling out a set of keys to retrieve ink and pen from a locked drawer. "How will you do that?" I ask.

"It's best if you're not privy to the details," he answers, already engaged in the task of recording the information I'd shared. "I'm sure you understand that it's for your safety. None of us can forget Nathan Hale, of course."

I flinch at the reference to the Continental Army captain. He had volunteered for the treacherous mission of going behind enemy lines to assemble information before the Battle of Harlem Heights. Despite the fact that he was disguised as a Dutch schoolmaster, the British recognized him and captured him on Long Island Sound while he was trying to get back into American territory. Then-commander General Howe ordered that Nathan Hale should be executed for espionage, and he was hanged.

I decide not to address this comment about Mr. Hale; after all, what can I say about the tragedy, other than insisting that it doesn't influence my decision to act now? "Mr. Townsend, I'm not asking for your protection. If it isn't obvious to you, I already take enormous risks in obtaining information for the cause, and even larger ones by coming to your shop alone. I expect that you trust me as I trust you."

He looks up from his letter writing. "It isn't a matter of trust, Miss Morris. It's a matter of keeping you safe."

"Safe? Why do you think ignorance will keep me safe?"

He stares at me, scrutinizing me as if the answer to my question lies in my features. "You do realize that more knowledge equates to more risk?"

"Haven't I made abundantly clear my intentions to help the Revolution? Haven't I already proven my tolerance—perhaps even appetite—for risk?"

Breathing deeply, he gestures for me to join him behind the counter. He dips his pen in the ink and begins writing, but nothing appears on the page. "It seems as though your ink well is dry," I comment.

"No, Miss Morris. The well is full of special ink prepared by an expert, James Jay."

The only Jay I know is John Jay, the Continental Congress delegate, and I wonder if the Jay to which Mr. Townsend refers is related. But now is not the time to inquire. "How does it work?" I ask.

"Only the intended recipient will be able to read the lettering by applying a specific stain to the paper. My words are otherwise invisible, and for all intents and purposes, this is a plain sheet of paper."

"Will you name your source in this letter?"

"Not exactly—this letter will have the additional protection of being in code."

"Even my name?"

"Oh yes."

"I have a code name, then?" I ask, enjoying the idea that I'm part of a scheme that includes the famous General Washington—that I'm so essential, I must be given a secret name.

His cheeks redden as he answers, "I refer to you as 'Agent 355.'"

I try not to reveal my disappointment at this rather plebeian choice. "I see. Does it have a meaning, beyond the mere number?"

"Yes," he says, with a small smile. "355 means lady."

"So you could be referring to any woman." I no longer hide my disappointment.

"No, it can only refer to you. I use the code number 701 to refer to a regular woman. But you aren't a 701. You are *the* 355, the quintessential *lady*, an accomplished young woman from an affluent family, well-versed in music, literature, needlework—"

"All useless skills."

"You didn't let me finish. You are accomplished, but also an uncommon *lady*—fiercely intelligent, well-read as any teacher, undeniably brave, selfless, and above all, good."

It is my turn to blush. I don't know how to respond to this rush of compliments, so heartfelt and unlike the empty flattery tossed about by the British and society folks. Instead, I blurt out another question. "How will you get this sheet of paper to General Washington without crossing over the battle lines to reach him?"

He seems relieved at the change of subject. "This sheet will be placed in a large sheaf of plain paper. A client who owns a business in Long Island or his messenger will travel to New York

City, ostensibly to buy supplies from my shop, including the sheaf of paper containing my message. He will take the paper home, and another individual will procure the specific sheet from his business. From there, it will pass into the hands of one of Washington's lieutenants capable of reading the invisible ink and interpreting the code. Hopefully they'll be able to put a stop to the counterfeiting before it even begins."

*How close my work will pass to the center of the fight,* I think. My heart races at this notion. "Meaning General Washington *himself* will learn the secret I uncovered?"

"He will indeed. After his officer in charge of intelligence, Benjamin Tallmadge, reads it first, of course." A wide smile transforms his face, and I see the handsome young man beneath his heavy, solemn exterior. "Welcome to the Culper Ring."

# CHAPTER 6

December 4, 1779
New York, New York

I allow another colonel—a Colonel Phillips, I believe—to swirl me around the dance floor, and I giggle as though I'm enjoying myself. In truth, I loathe the feel of his gloved hands at my waist, and it takes all my strength to keep from running straight out of the room. But I know that if I decline to dance with this man and chatter with him and his fellow officers, I will have no access to my actual target tonight: Major André. So dance I must.

We pass my parents watching the dance floor, their faces beaming at the sight of their daughter—their only child—swept along in the arms of a British officer. They've been visibly delighted with the change in my behavior over these past few months, and I feel heartsick at how I must deceive them for the Continental cause. Yet, just as I must engage in this reprehensible game of flirtation with the British, there is no other way to serve the Revolution than to mislead my parents. Because, as I'm now certain, the information I gather is critical to the war. The report I delivered to Mr. Townsend—which traveled from Robert to Washington himself—halted the British plan to counterfeit currency before it even began, and the general hungers for more high-level intelligence from us. From *me*.

The minuet ends, and I accept Colonel Phillips's invitation for a glass of punch. As I stand among officers and young ladies sipping at the lukewarm drink, the conversation drifts to a soiree planned for next weekend at the home of the Fowlers. The ladies chat about the planned festivities—a round of charades mixed in with the usual activities—but the men are strangely quiet.

I turn to my dance partner and ask in a coy tone, "Will you be able to join us next weekend at the Fowlers', Colonel Phillips?"

Phillips looks at his fellow officers, as if asking permission to answer. Two of them shrug while the other remains blank, so he says, "I probably shouldn't say too much, except that we have just learned it's unlikely our battalion will be back in town by then. We have orders to leave in the morning."

A quiet gasp passes through the group of women, many of whom have enjoyed the attentions of the Redcoats, even formed real attachments over their months of occupation. "Will you return?" one asks, her voice quivering.

The fair officer with whom she'd been spending time—with eyebrows and eyelashes so blond they almost appear white—draws close to her and says, "We don't yet know when we'll return from Charleston. But of course, we can always exchange letters."

None of the women seems to have registered the slip about the British destination, and none of the officers seem to care. Why would they? After all, what harm could come from sharing military plans with a gaggle of young ladies? What interest could we possibly have in the details of the war?

As the conversation devolves into the young ladies' supplying their addresses to the soldiers, I withdraw. My mind is racing. Can I get this information to Mr. Townsend tonight? I'm fairly certain that his contact in Long Island has a visit scheduled to his shop tomorrow, and if I can inform Mr. Townsend of the British plan to depart New York for South Carolina, the Continental Army may be able to head them off at the pass.

I survey the party. My parents and the older folks mill about the drawing room and parlor and gather around the food in the dining room. They seem engrossed in their own discussions. Couples continue to spin to the musicians' allemande, but I notice that a few have started to drift off the floor as news of the British departure begins to spread. Could I sneak through the servants' door near the kitchen to reach the alley? If so, I could run behind the homes on this street without detection.

Making myself small, I edge past revelers and keep to the shadows as I walk to the back hallway leading to the kitchen. The cook and her two maids are busy refilling trays of meats and fruits on a work table, and they take no notice of me as I slide out the door, which is already ajar to allow smoke from the kitchen fires to waft out of the house.

I cannot risk fetching my cloak before my departure, so I brave the night air with my arms exposed. Scanning the street from the vantage point of the alley, I see that it's mercifully empty. I step out into the dark, icy night, and run.

I knock and knock on the shop door, but no one answers. *How stupid,* I think. Why did I think Robert would be at his store at this late hour? He's probably at home, wherever that is. How could I have been so reckless, leaving the party and racing through the city streets in my velvet evening gown unescorted, for nothing?

But then, through the window, I see light in the back of the store. The illumination grows brighter, and I realize someone is approaching, candle in hand. I whisper a prayer that the person is Mr. Townsend, not some suspicious stranger.

"Miss Morris, come in, come in. The night is frigid, and you have no coat."

Mr. Townsend guides me into the shop, which isn't much warmer than the street. "What on earth are you doing here at this hour?" he asks, fetching a blanket from behind the counter to wrap around me, covering my formal gown.

My teeth are chattering, but I stammer out, "I have crucial information for you to give your contact tomorrow."

"It couldn't wait?"

"No, I don't believe so." I inhale deeply and steady my speech. "I've just heard General Clinton has ordered that Major André and his men leave the city for Charleston in the morning."

"How can that be? That would mean that they've essentially abandoned their attempts to retake Philadelphia." His tone borders on disbelief.

"I know what I heard." I try not to take offense at his incredulity, reminding myself that it does seem inconceivable that the British would give up the fight for Philadelphia. Last summer, the British were forced to evacuate Philadelphia after holding the Continental capital since September of 1777. By all accounts, the Redcoats have been scheming to get it back ever since.

"Could they really have changed their focus to the South?"

I don't back down. "The officers explicitly said they had orders to leave for Charleston in the morning, and anyway, it makes sense with other things I've overheard. Just this week, a group of officers had a spirited conversation about the rumors that there are great numbers of Loyalists in the Southern colonies."

He nods slowly, allowing the news and all its implications to settle in. "Perhaps the British are planning on drawing southern Loyalists into their forces as they launch an offensive in the South."

"Perhaps," I say. "I've also heard rumbling about forces amassing near Savannah."

He pauses. "General Washington needs to know this as soon as possible. He may be able to attack some of the British ships as they sail south, but if not, at the very least, he can forewarn the southern units of the Continental Army, and they can prepare."

He turns to me, his expression soft and concerned. "You've done a tremendous service for the Revolution, but I don't like the risk you've taken coming here tonight."

"Mr. Townsend—" I begin, but he interrupts me.

"Would it be improper for me to invite you to call me Robert? Mr. Townsend sounds so ceremonious, and the work in which we are engaged . . ." He stops, uncertain how to proceed.

I finish for him. "Unites us in an uncommon way? Makes the usual formalities seem discordant?"

His mouth curves gently into a small smile. "Exactly."

"I would be honored to call you Robert. But only if you agree to call me Elizabeth."

# CHAPTER 7

We laugh at the finicky requests of the elderly woman who has just left Townsend's Dry Goods. As always, women come in asking for all sorts of obscure or inaccessible items, such as thread in a particular shade of azure or foodstuffs that are popular with the troops and therefore out of reach for regular, non-military folks. But as our merriment subsides, Robert's face turns unexpectedly serious. "What's troubling you?" I ask, smoothing the skirt of my simple linen dress, one of two that I wear on market days.

"I worry that your visits will be noticed," he says, not meeting my gaze.

"By whom?"

"By anyone sympathetic to the British, and who happens to be aware of my family history." He chortles. "Or maybe your family, or their servants."

"Why would my visits draw anyone's attention? I am simply a regular customer, visiting your establishment to purchase your excellent silk threads for my embroidery. You do have regular customers, don't you?" I ask with a playful smile.

Even though Major André and his men left New York City over five months ago for their attack on Charleston—a campaign that my intelligence was unable to stop, despite our best efforts—I find myself manufacturing reasons to see this kind, serious man, as the British departure leaves me with little to report. His quiet fortitude and fervent belief in freedom and equality mirror my own, and make the company of others seem empty. Whenever opportunity arises for a market visit, I sneak over to his shop to see if I can wring a smile from his pensive face. Of course, at home, I've had to cover my tracks by actually undertaking mass quantities of needlework projects, much to my private dismay.

"I do have regular customers, of course. But . . ." He trails off, and I see that familiar flush on his cheeks as he stares back down at his ledger.

"But what?"

"But I don't have any other customers that are so uncommonly . . . noticeable."

"What do you mean?" I know exactly what he's insinuating, but I pretend otherwise. We have been circling around the topic of our feelings for each other for some weeks now, and it seems I may need to force the issue. He will not say plainly what he plainly feels—what we both feel. But no matter how "uncommon" Robert finds me, I cannot be the first to profess my emotions. My unorthodoxy does not stretch that far.

"So uncommonly pretty," he says, his face turning a shade of red so deep that it appears purple.

Even though I am well-pleased, I'm uncertain how to reply. I have little experience with gentlemen, other than the pretending I do with the British, devoid of any sincere emotion. And I am no coquette.

"Well," I say, keeping my eyes fixed on the tips of my shoes. "Perhaps the usual reason could explain my visits to the shop."

"What is the usual reason?" He sounds genuinely perplexed.

"Courting," I answer and lift my eyes to meet his.

I had believed that his cheeks could not redden further, but I was wrong. "Courting?" he stammers, then collects himself and continues. "Would a young lady of your station really court a man of mine?"

"If she cared for him, of course," I answer. "And anyway, you come from a perfectly respectable station. Your family owns extensive land on Long Island, and you run your own successful business."

"S—so, is that why you come to my shop, Elizabeth?"

I force myself to hold his gaze, to show him that I am unafraid to embrace this connection. "In part."

I watch as his fingers move across the polished wood of the counter toward mine. For a brief moment, our fingertips touch, and our eyes meet. But then the intensity of his gaze overwhelms me, and I blurt out, "But there is another reason I came today."

Disappointment registers on his face, and he withdraws his hand. "There is?"

"Major André and his men will arrive back in New York tomorrow. My parents received word from one of the few officers that remain in the city. The British want us to prepare our homes for hosting again."

Robert is quiet. When he doesn't speak for a long moment, I say, "I thought you'd be pleased that my source of information has returned. You've mentioned that General Washington has been grumbling about the lack of intelligence coming from the Culper Ring since André left for Charleston, that he might even disband it."

"Of course. But with the return of André comes the return of your involvement with them. I loathe the thought of you consorting with the British—dancing with them, dining with them, even talking with them. I cannot stop thinking about the night we first met, when that awful colonel was attempting to interfere with you." He takes a deep breath. "I don't want you to compromise yourself to obtain information."

"You needn't worry, Robert. Even as a woman, I'm capable of protecting myself against British advances while obtaining information—and not compromising myself while doing so. There have been no more instances of the sort you witnessed the night we first met, and there never will be again. I won't be so foolhardy."

"I know you're capable, Elizabeth, and you're the antithesis of foolish. It's just that—that . . ." He pauses. "I care about you too much to risk you."

# CHAPTER 8

July 20, 1780
New York, New York

The largest of the summer balls unfolds before me—this one hosted by several families at the assembly hall, because no one home can accommodate so large an affair. But my mind is not on the festooned revelers who swirl past me. Instead, I'm thinking about the success of the past few weeks and a special evening Robert and I shared in its wake. And I'm smiling to myself.

Immediately upon the British soldiers' return to New York— riding high on their capture of Charleston—rumors began to surface about a French fleet sailing to our shores to aid the Continental Army. But no one knew where these ships would land, not even General Washington. I listened to many conversations in which British officers speculated about the location, and I learned that General Clinton planned to send troops and ships to attack the French on the Rhode Island coast, where he believed they would make shore. The moment I heard this, I raced to tell Robert. My intelligence led to an intricate plot in which Washington leaked false information to the British, indicating that he planned to take back New York while Clinton's troops were in Rhode Island, and thereby prompting Clinton to turn back from Rhode Island, giving the French unimpeded access to our shore. This victory was one that Robert and I celebrated in the privacy of his shop after closing time, with a toast and our first real kiss.

I return to the present moment, wondering whether another opportunity for espionage will reveal itself this evening. At several recent gatherings and dinners, I've noticed a certain smugness adopted by the British officers, even beyond the swagger with which they returned from Charleston, a swagger that was not diminished by their failure to intercept the French in Rhode Island. *What is happening,* I wonder, *to justify this new confidence?* Will I learn its source tonight?

I find the men to be strangely silent once I'm in their presence. Several seemingly innocent queries placed with the usual cadre of officers yield nothing, and I begin to despair of learning some tightly held secret. Frustrated at the British recalcitrance, I stand near the ballroom door with a group of young women I've known my whole life, talking, as usual, about nothing. It is then that Major André himself sidles up to me and asks for a dance.

The other women raise eyebrows and whisper among themselves as the musicians strike the first few chords of a minuet. Although the polished, attractive Major André is notoriously flirtatious with most of the young ladies, he only dances with a select few. He rests one hand on my waist and another on my shoulder, and I find myself nervous in the presence of the central British intelligence officer, the man with spies and schemes abounding, the man upon whom *I* have been spying. Will he sniff out the intruder in his midst?

"How is it that we've often been in each other's company over these past months, and yet we've never danced?" He poses a question that I'm sure he's asked countless times to countless women.

"I think it must be because you've never asked, sir."

He guffaws, a rather jolting sound coming from his compact mouth. "Nicely said, Miss. . . ? Apologies for not knowing your name."

"Miss Morris, sir, and please don't apologize. I have the advantage in that, while there are many young Loyalist women in this town, there is only one you."

He laughs again, drawing the attention of the ever-present audience on the periphery of the dance floor. "I'm glad to learn we're in the company of such witty Loyalist women."

"Loyalist women who are excited to have you back. We welcomed the news from Charleston, but we're so pleased that you all have returned to New York, and that you're winning this fight."

"I appreciate your support, Miss Morris. Our victories in New York and Charleston are only the beginning. We will soon have the entire coast at our disposal."

*Here it is,* I think. This innuendo must be the source of the heightened British confidence I've observed. But what exactly is going to yield the coast to the British? I'm so close to the secreted truth, and I cannot allow the opportunity to pass, even though it's risky to pursue the information I seek.

While I muse on the best course, I respond with the flattery he expects. "I have no doubt of it, Major André."

Do I dare ask him the sort of questions I've posed to the others? Will he suspect me? Maybe he asked me to dance because he suspects me already.

The major continues, "Don't think that it will be easy, Miss Morris. Although the Continental Army is a gaggle of rag-tag upstarts in comparison to our well-trained troops, they have the fury of the indignant, unwarranted though that may be. Still, I have no doubt that we will prevail."

Putting aside Robert's ongoing concerns about my safety, I decide to take the risk. It may be my only chance.

"It sounds as though securing the coast—I think that's what you said—" I add with false uncertainty, "will be instrumental in the British success, yes?"

"Ah, you've been listening," he teases. "Yes, we have plans in motion that will deliver the seaboard to us. Now I cannot tell you more, even though you are a dutiful citizen of the Crown. I can, however, assure you that you have no reason to worry."

"I'd never worry with you in charge, Major André. You will undoubtedly ensure that our land is fully restored to British rule soon. And I wouldn't understand the details of your plans anyway."

"I don't doubt that, dear girl, and I wouldn't tax you so. But be assured that we have a leader of the Continental Army in alignment with our views, and that will help our cause immeasurably."

I nod blankly, and turn the conversation to the sorts of entertainment I imagine he enjoys in England. We thus converse on an utterly inane topic, as I turn the information he's shared round and round in my mind.

"Those were his precise words?" Robert asks the next afternoon, his voice raised excitedly.

I repeat them. "Yes, verbatim, André said: 'We have a leader of the Continental Army in alignment with our views, and that will help our cause immeasurably.' This person must be in one of the commanding roles somewhere along the coast, given the context."

Robert shakes his head in disbelief. "Washington has a traitor in his midst! And a senior officer, at that."

"So it would seem."

"But who?"

"I've been thinking through every possibility, and I would venture to guess that leader is tied to one of the waterfront forts. Perhaps West Point? I understand that its location, on a sharp bend in the Hudson River, would allow it to dictate ships' access to the river, and thus the state. And we know how important New York is to the success of either side."

"Yes, it's very strategic. Although I don't think the fort currently has a commander."

"Maybe the leader that André mentioned is attempting to secure the command."

Robert nods and reaches for my hand. "You've outdone yourself, Elizabeth."

I feel my cheeks flush with his compliment, as I hold his hand in mine. "Thank you, Robert."

Despite his praise, his expression is somber, and he says, "But I worry about the position in which you might've placed yourself to acquire this information."

"What do you mean?"

"André has a reputation."

"He did not dishonor me, Robert." I squeeze his hand. "I know it may be inconceivable to you—you who don't think less of women's intellect—but almost every other man believes he can tell anything to a woman without repercussions, assuming our inherent inability to understand. And such men don't need special encouragement to reveal their secrets—even a spymaster."

# CHAPTER 9

September 18, 1780
New York, New York

My heart races as I pad down the stairs. I carry my shoes and am careful to avoid the step with the notorious creak, and yet, the wooden stairs screech as I descend. I pause, wanting to ensure I haven't roused Officer Randolph, who has commandeered my father's study on the first floor as his bed chamber ever since he returned from Charleston. Hearing nothing other than my father's light snore, I continue downstairs. I know I should wait a full minute before crossing the entryway to the kitchen, but I am eager. This new information cannot wait until market day.

*If I can make it to the back hallway without detection, then I should be clear to exit out the servants' door,* I think. Placing one foot in front of the other with care, I creep across the foyer, past the dining room and toward the kitchen, still hot from the summer warmth and the dying embers in the ovens. Once inside the kitchen, I reach for the small parcel I've hidden in a cupboard and walk toward the door. It is then that I hear a noise.

I spin around, only to find Officer Randolph standing in the doorway to the kitchen. My heart beats wildly as I realize I've been caught.

"What are you doing?" he asks, rubbing his bleary eyes.

Hoping that my voice sounds light, I offer my prepared response as I pull my robe tighter around me to ensure my sheer white nightgown is fully covered. "Just looking for a late night bite to eat from the larder. Would you like something as well?"

The slight, exacting soldier stares at me, and I'm not certain whether he doubts me or is simply tired and confused. "It's more dawn than midnight," he says. Smoothing his unruly curls, he cranes his neck to look at the tall case clock in the foyer. "It's nearly three o'clock in the morning. Plenty strange for you to wander downstairs at this hour, Miss Morris."

"I suppose I didn't eat enough for dinner." I stroll to the larder and pull out a hunk of cheese and the remains of the day's bread. "Can I offer you some?"

Shaking his head, he stares at me quizzically, finally saying, "No, thank you. We have an early morning, and I'm not well pleased to have been awoken. We are trained to be on high alert for the rebels, you know."

I freeze. Did he just say the word *rebels*? I force myself to react calmly, even light-heartedly, as if he could not possibly affix that label to me. But now I wonder if he harbors suspicions about me.

"My apologies, Colonel," I say, then glance around the room. "There are no rebels here, as you can see, only me. And I did endeavor to be quiet, but I'm sorry that I woke you."

With a final glance, he takes his leave, and I am forced to go through the charade of eating until I estimate that he's had enough time to fall back asleep. Parcel in hand, I open the back door as slowly and silently as possible, and creep outside. Standing against the wall of the house, behind a shed used for tools, I put my father's pants and shirt over my nightdress, slide on a pair of boots, and tuck my hair in a hat, hoping I'll be mistaken for an errand boy working for an early-morning business. And then I run.

"What in the name of God are you doing here at this hour, Elizabeth? You know it's not safe," Robert whispers as he guides me into his shop.

I start to talk, but he places a finger over my lips. "We shouldn't be seen in here, and the light gives us away. It's too suspicious. Let's head upstairs."

For all the time that Robert and I have spent together, for all the secrets we have shared and feelings we have confessed, he has never invited me into his rooms over the shop. An unmarried man and woman alone together—particularly in the dead of night—breaches every boundary of propriety.

I am still breathless from my dash down the pitch-dark streets, so I take a moment to sit in the chair he offers me in his dining area. As he lights a few lamps around the room, I see that his kitchen, dining room, and parlor are essentially one large chamber, tidy and clean, but very plain. No Chippendale furniture or John Singleton Copley portraits here. The sole hint of any sort of decoration or indulgence is the stacks of books on the table and near the cushioned chair drawn close to the fireplace. I glimpse a few of the titles, some of which are familiar: William Camden's *Britannia*, a historical account of early England; Henry Home's *Principles of Equity*, a study of various legal systems; and a particular favorite of mine, John Locke's *Two Treatises of Government*.

He finally settles into the carved wooden chair next to me, takes my hand in his, and asks, "What's happened?"

"I believe Major André has left New York this very evening to meet his turncoat general," I say. "I overheard the critical facts from André himself at a church luncheon this afternoon, which was attended by soldiers and citizens alike. As the luncheon progressed, I noticed an increase in pointed glances, congratulatory back slaps, and surreptitious toasts among the officers, which heightened my suspicions that the plan to which André first alluded nearly two months ago was in motion."

"Did you hear anyone reference the name of the leader? A particular general, perhaps?" he asks. While he'd gotten word to Washington about the notion of this traitorous leader, no evidence had yet emerged about his exact identity, only guesses. Robert and I have a suspicion as to who this man may be, but haven't managed to find proof to implicate him. We know that identifying the traitor is of the utmost importance: If the British could capture the strategic fort of West Point through the treachery of one of Washington's key men, it would be an unimaginable coup. General Washington might never recover.

"No, there was no confirmation of a name. But I did overhear André say that he was heading north for a few days—that he was leaving tonight after his 'send-off dinner,' as he described it. And West Point is, of course—"

"North." Robert finishes the sentence for me.

"Yes. Then, not five minutes later, I swear I heard one of his men mention White Plains, which would be on the way to West Point. I am guessing that André has a rendezvous with this traitor, and that they are finalizing the details of the handover of West Point to the British."

"Which would give the British an enormous advantage over the Continental Army in New York—and beyond."

"Exactly. Now do you understand why I had to come? We need to get this information to Washington now, so he can stop the meeting from ever happening and arrest this newly appointed general as a traitor."

"You're right to come, Elizabeth, although I hate the dangers to which you must subject yourself. I hope you didn't have to suffer through another dance with André to procure this information."

"No. Thankfully, he hasn't asked me again."

Robert appears visibly relieved, but then his brow furrows. "My contact isn't due here for two days, so I'll have to take the message myself to his conduit to Washington."

"No, Robert. That's too big a risk."

"Not if it appears as though I'm simply visiting my family in Long Island."

"Can you safely relay the information to Washington from there?"

"I'll have to hand it over directly to the conduit at his business in Long Island, which will be a bit tricky, but I believe I can manage it. From there, the conduit should be able to get the message to Washington at his headquarters in New Jersey through his normal channels." He squeezes my hand and leans in to gently kiss me. "I cannot allow you to be the only member of the Culper Ring to take these enormous risks."

He pauses for a moment and adds, "Do you still believe that we've identified the right man?"

"Yes—with his recent appointment at West Point and his wife's family ties to the Loyalists, Major André in particular . . . it just can't be a coincidence."

And so we found our traitor, or at least we believed we had: Gen. Benedict Arnold.

# CHAPTER 10

"Damn shame!" My father slaps the newspaper down on the dining room table, causing the Wedgwood china to vibrate. I've just entered the room for breakfast, and I cannot imagine what would prompt him to swear, an unprecedented act in my experience. "This will be horrific for business."

"Language, Richard," my mother scolds. But she doesn't comment on the source of his outrage. She continues stirring her tea.

"What's happened?" I ask.

"Remember that Major André, dear? Very nice fellow," she says.

"Yes," I venture warily.

"Well," says my father, "it seems that his primary job wasn't aiding General Clinton after all, as he led us to believe. He was serving as an intelligence officer. Gathering up rebel secrets and the like, if you can imagine it. Apparently, he'd struck some sort of deal for a Continental general to switch sides to the British, and he was found behind enemy lines after a meeting with this general."

"Really? How on earth did he get caught?" I ask.

"It seems he stumbled into a roadblock when he was leaving his meeting in the countryside," he answers, and I realize that the roadblock had been erected based on my report about André's meeting and whereabouts. "When he was arrested, Major André had very damaging papers on his person—a map of West Point and a document signed by the general who ran the fort." He turns to my mother. "What was his name?"

"Arnold. A Gen. Benedict Arnold."

"Yes, that's it."

My heart pounds in my chest, and the room begins to sway. All my suspicions have proven accurate, and I know—without a shred of doubt—that it was my information, delivered to Robert just days ago, that upended this plot.

"What is it, dear?" my mother asks, noticing a change in my expression.

"A lot of the girls fancied Major André. Perhaps our Elizabeth is no exception," my father comments, almost humorously.

I compose myself, and answer as if I am still the old Elizabeth, the innocent girl who could exchange quips with her father and resist her mother's attempts to make her more marriageable, the young woman who preferred staying home in the evening with a book by the fire to attending a bustling party. I barely remember her anymore. Now I'm a new Elizabeth, a spy for the Continental Army who deceives her family and friends in order to pry information from the British. "Don't be silly, Father. He was too much of a fop for my taste."

"Oh, Elizabeth! We will never find you a suitable husband with that attitude. And I thought you'd really begun to change," my mother says.

I sit down in my usual chair across from them at the table, reach for a piece of bread as if it is a normal morning, and only then pick up the newspaper as casually as I can. "So what happened to Major André and this Arnold fellow? Are they both under arrest?"

"Ah, there's a bit of good news there," my father says. "It seems that Major André was arrested before the rebels fully understood that this Arnold fellow was about to betray them, and so one of their colonels notified Arnold that they had a British officer in custody with papers bearing his name. Arnold, of course, understood that it was only a matter of time before the rebels comprehended that he was in league with Major André, and came to arrest him as well."

"What did Arnold do?" I ask, holding my breath, praying that they got Arnold despite his foreknowledge.

"Well, this gaffe on the part of the Continental colonel gave Arnold time to escape before the rebels realized he was part of the scheme. Arnold reached the British, and they now have him to use as an asset, even though they lost the chance to take West Point." He chuckles. "Imagine Washington's face when he arrived at the fort expecting to see General Arnold, only to discover he'd fled in the nick of time."

"But poor Major André, he's still imprisoned." My mother sighs. "And he was such a nice gentleman."

"Yes, he was," I answer without thinking. My mind is focused elsewhere, churning with questions that would shock and dismay my parents if they knew.

What does it mean that Major André was caught, but General Arnold escaped? Will Arnold realize that André stepped into our trap? If so, how long will it be before the British begin to hunt down the spies who gathered that information? I am haunted by the thought that Arnold knows about the Culper Ring.

I am riddled with fear, but cannot show it. I must proceed apace with normal life—as normal a life as can be led in wartime—continuing with the daily cycle of a lady's activities and attending the required social gatherings. Otherwise, I risk drawing attention to myself, and scrutiny is something I can ill afford.

For weeks, the lavish parties continue despite the mourning the hanging of Major André on General Washington's orders. I attend these soirees, but do not make any inquiries or listen where I am not wanted. Instead, I dance when asked; I drink when libations are proffered; I engage in ladylike conversations about the weather, people's health, and the evening's festivities; and I wish to be forgotten.

That does not mean I can entirely close my ears, of course. I hear Officer Randolph talk in my parents' home about the desire for revenge over the spoiled plot and the death of Major André. I attend to the murmurings on the high street, in the church and the park, and over afternoon tea, all whispering about Arnold's hunt for the spies who exposed the plan that he and André concocted. I feel the threat of being discovered everywhere, even when I am in the privacy of my bedchamber. And I begin to wonder if that threat is real or imagined.

I hear the sound of something falling or breaking, and I sit up with a jolt. I gaze around my bedroom, seeing only the outline of my bureau against the background of the moon and nothing out of the ordinary. I decide I'd been dreaming, and try to return to sleep. A few minutes later, I hear the noise again, realizing that it's the hard strike of a rock on my window.

Wrapping my robe around me, I walk to the window and peer down onto our side yard. I see a lanky figure near the hedge, and I recognize the silhouette immediately. Robert.

Thank God.

I light a candle and raise my hand to indicate that I've seen him. Motioning for him to join me in the back yard, I creep down the stairs, praying that I do not wake Officer Randolph again. An excuse of a late night repast will not be accepted a second time.

I pass through the back door and into the garden behind the house unnoticed. This is the province of the servants, littered with clothes lines, washing bins, and carts. Their belongings will shield us from any wakeful inhabitants of the house, as will the small grove of trees.

"Robert," I say, racing to his side.

He wraps his arms around me, and for the first time in weeks, I feel safe and known. "I'm so sorry I've left you out here on your own. I've wanted to knock on your parents' door so many times these past weeks," he says.

"Hush." I place my finger on his lips, relishing the soft texture of his skin. "That would have been foolish. For us both. That's why I stayed away from your store."

His face is shadowy in the dark, but in the low light of the moon, I can see his eyes looking into mine. His voice cracks with emotion as he says, "Your discovery allowed Washington to stop the British takeover of West Point and brought down their chief spy."

"That's what I had hoped."

"But . . . at what cost?"

"What do you mean?" I ask, fearing that I already know the answer.

"You must know. As a Continental Army general, Arnold had been informed about the existence of the Culper Ring, although he hadn't been told the names of its members. But he realizes that we're the ones to have uncovered his plot, and he is circling around us, drawing close. I'm terribly worried that he'll identify us soon, and give the British our names."

"I've been hearing whispers about Arnold's desperation to find the spies, but I didn't realize they were near to discovering us." All the terror that had been wound tightly within me over the past weeks releases, and I begin crying. "What are we going to do?"

Robert wipes away the tears streaming down my cheeks, never loosening his hold on me. "I have a plan, but I don't want you to think me presumptuous."

"I would never think that, Robert. I know you, and I know you have my well-being at heart, and—and I know how you feel about me."

He stares into my eyes, and with his finger, traces the path of my drying tears. I allow my cheek to rest in his palm, and for a long moment, I feel at peace.

Then he says, "Elizabeth, will you marry me?"

No matter my assurances about his plan, I am stunned. In my sphere, marriage is a decision that's made by a family, not an individual. *But,* I remind myself, *I am operating far outside the normal sphere.* And with sudden certainty, I know this is the right course. Life with this serious, moral man will never be the easy life of plenty my parents envision for me, but it will be the life of goodness and integrity and purpose for which I long.

He fills my silence with words. "We could marry and then leave New York together as a couple—before they identify us. I've mapped out a way for us to make it safely to New Jersey or Connecticut, where General Washington could protect us. Of course, I know this isn't the normal manner of courting and engagement, as I haven't approached your parents. They would never approve anyway. You wouldn't have the formal wedding and party that you deserve, and we'd have to sneak away in the dead of night afterward, but—"

Again, I place my finger on his lips. "Shhh, my dearest Robert. I will marry you. The details of how we go about our union are unimportant to me. All that matters is that I will become your wife."

# CHAPTER 11

October 25, 1780
New York, New York

The tiny stone chapel of St. Paul's, tucked away in a field on Broadway, is beautiful in its spareness. Gleaming white walls glow in the golden, late morning sun, and the burnished oak pews and altar only heighten the illumination. The church is empty, save for us three, and it seems fitting that the minister will marry us in this place which was claimed by the early supporters of the Revolution.

Robert and I stand before the altar, hand in hand, the folds of my simple lilac gown pooling at our feet. We face the minister he knows from childhood, a man secretly sympathetic to the cause of the Revolution even though he leads a Loyalist congregation. Robert had once considered approaching him about undertaking intelligence work for the cause, but once he understood the breadth of the minister's pacifist leanings, he abandoned the notion.

The minister has warned us that the ceremony will unite us before God, but not before the government, whichever one ends up winning this war. According to the law, my parents have the right to deny me permission to marry, and we had not the time nor consent to post the banns—our declaration of intent to marry—at any church, as is tradition and rule. It's only been twelve hours since Robert's proposal, after all. But we do not care.

I glance at Robert, who stares at me with a wide grin of disbelief, as if I might disappear in an instant, like a specter. I smile back at him, to assure him that I am indeed flesh and blood, and I am his.

The minister begins. "We gather here today in the sight of God to join together this man and this woman in holy matrimony." He continues with the familiar litany about the meaning of the sacrament, but I only half listen. I'm too transfixed by the glorious smile on Robert's face and the happiness in his eyes; I can only imagine that I appear the same.

"Elizabeth Morris, wilt thou have this man to be thy wedded husband, to live together after God's ordinance, in the holy estate of matrimony? Wilt thou obey him, serve him, love, honor, and keep him in sickness and in health, and forsaking all others, keep thee only unto him, so long as ye both shall live?"

"I will."

"Robert Townsend, wilt thou have this woman to be thy wedded wife to live together after God's ordinance, in the holy estate of matrimony? Wilt thou love, honor, and keep her in sickness and in health, and forsaking all others, keep thee only unto her, so long as ye both shall live?"

"I will."

He hands Robert a ring, a simple band of silver with a lovely flower design along its rim. As Robert slides it on my finger, he repeats after the minister, "With this ring, I thee wed, with my body, I thee worship, and with all my worldly goods, I thee endow."

After the minister's final blessing, we exit by the side door of St. Paul's, daring to hold hands as we walk down the lanes to Townsend's Dry Goods Shop. The store, which I have visited often in both daylight and moonlight, seems different now that I am Robert's wife. After he unlocks the door, he leads me upstairs to his rooms, which I have only ever visited at night. To my surprise, bouquets of blue asters, purple spotted bee balm, and goldenrod adorn the room, and their fragrant perfume fills the air.

As I turn toward Robert in delight, he says, "I cannot offer you much right now, but I wanted our wedding day to be as celebratory as I could make it."

"What you have offered me is all that I have ever wanted."

He pulls me close to him. "What you have offered me is more than I ever knew existed." Wrapping me in his arms, he engulfs me in a kiss, then leads me to his bedroom.

The sun wanes by late afternoon when I am preparing to leave Robert's shop, but the day is no less beautiful and bright. In Robert's arms, I listen as he whispers, "I don't want you to leave." His voice is thick with desire and regret.

"Neither do I," I whisper into his chest. Then, in an effort to sound more hopeful, I say, "But it will be only eight short hours until we rendezvous. And then we will be together forever."

"Those hours will be endless," he groans.

"I know. But you have much to do by way of packing for us. I'll have to slip out with only a small bag to avoid detection, so you'll have to prepare for us both. Then I'll be yours for all time."

"For all time," he echoes, a note of wonder in his voice. And he holds me in a long farewell kiss.

I walk the distance home in a euphoric daze. As I stroll, the remains of Trinity Church—whose steeple was once the tallest structure in the city—capture my attention, and I wonder when it will be reconstructed after the fire that razed much of the city. I cannot help but think that, despite the unorthodox nature of our marriage, a benevolent God would look kindly upon our union today.

As I approach my parents' home, I begin to worry. How will my parents react when they read my letter tomorrow morning, and they learn about my marriage and departure? Will they discover the hand I had in André's arrest and the upending of Arnold's plot? And what will the British do to my parents if their investigation reveals my involvement? Regardless of my worries, I know I cannot alert my mother and father too soon, or I risk ruining our plan. So I slide my wedding ring off my finger and hide it deep within a pocket in the folds of my skirt.

Pulling open the front door, I step inside to a scene I could have never imagined. My mother stands at the base of the entryway stairs, clutching the bannister, her cheeks wet with tears. My father's usually perfectly styled hair is askew, and he is arguing with an unfamiliar British officer who is surrounded by at least six of his men. Officer Randolph stands behind them, his arms crossed and a self-satisfied expression on his face. The commotion halts when they see me.

My mother screams: "Run, Elizabeth, run!"

Before I attempt to leave, I meet my father's gaze, and see within his deep blue eyes an excess of anguish and helplessness. I hesitate for a second, and in that momentary pause, one of the men grasps my hand just as I'm about to flee through the door.

As he grips both my arms and yanks them behind my back, the senior officer marches to my side and announces, "Elizabeth Morris, you are under arrest for treason."

# CHAPTER 12

I am taken from my family home in shackles. The British march me down the high street, announcing to anyone who will listen that they have captured the spy responsible for the betrayal of Major André and, ultimately, his death. We pass neighbors and family friends of many years, and the astonishment on their expressions as they watch me in chains makes real the hellacious fate awaiting me: the HMS *Jersey*.

Everyone in New York has heard stories about the notorious prison ship where rebels are held and the appalling conditions yield a life expectancy of only a few months. Consequently, as the British soldiers take me by carriage to the docks at Wallabout Bay, I think I know what terrors to expect once I'm on board. But I am wrong. No newspaper article or overheard conversation could prepare me for this reality.

After I climb up the ladder to board, I am transferred into the hands of the notorious Commissary Joshua Loring. Even in the society circles of New York, I'd heard talk of this reprehensible creature, who enjoys inflicting the harshest of conditions on his prisoners and hoards the meager food and drink allotted to them to then trade on the black market for his own gain. Loring laughs when he learns he'll have a woman on board—"a novelty for your fellow prisoners and a plaything for them as well," he comments—and passes me off to his second-in-command. It is this man who pushes me down the flight of nearly vertical stairs into the hull of the *Jersey*.

If hell could take earthly form, it would resemble this ship. Half-dead bodies are strewn about the rough wooden floor in various states of undress, as there are neither beds nor hammocks, not even benches. Those prisoners still able to stand or sit upright against the inwardly curving wood-slat walls are racked with cough and covered with scabs. They're dressed in what I could only describe as rags. There are so many men in the cramped, windowless space that those clinging to life overlap with cadavers on the floor, and the rodents scurry over them. But worse than the illness, worse than the crowding, worse than the degenerated state of the prisoners, worse than the constant moaning, is the smell, which contains elements of rotten food, decaying flesh, fetid water, men long unwashed, and some stench far worse than any single one of those.

I cower in the corner closest to the stairs, thinking that when the hatch above opens, at least I can catch a momentary rush of fresh air. The minutes elapse, then the hours, and the sealed hull darkens along with the passage of time. I still anticipate that gust, but the hatch never moves. As the air grows thicker and more foul in the growing gloom, I brace myself.

Night takes a firm hold, and the hull becomes almost pitch black. The prisoners are not allowed candles, of course, as fire might provide a means of escape, and thus the only illumination is the hint of moonlight that sneaks in through the gaps in the wooden slat walls. Exhaustion threatens to overwhelm me, although I know I cannot fall asleep, or I risk much greater vulnerability. Thoughts of Robert pervade my mind, and I weep silently in the blackness for the loss of the new life we were meant to embark upon this very night.

A thud sounds in the hull. I see the outline of a man approaching slowly, and I ready myself to retaliate. When he comes close enough that I can discern bits of his face and dress, I see a hollow-faced older man, his dark hair shot through with light gray, wearing a tattered Continental Army uniform.

"Do not come any closer," I hiss, wanting to warn him, but not to awaken the sleeping prisoners.

"I, I don't mean to scare you, Miss Morris. You are Elizabeth Morris, aren't you?"

How does this man know my name? It is hardly as if Loring's assistant introduced me before he shoved me down the stairs.

Panic surges through me. "Then don't approach me."

He takes a big step backward and whispers, "Can you hear me from this distance?"

I nod.

"The last thing in the world that I want to do is to frighten you. This place is terrifying enough on its own." He coughs, an unnerving, rattling sound. "You've done so much for our cause, and I simply want to offer my services to you. Limited though they may be in this gruesome place."

"What do you think I've done for your cause? And how do you know who I am?"

He gestures to four men standing behind him, who've silently gathered. "We have means of receiving information about the war, as well as letters and small parcels. And we have heard about what you did to stop Arnold and André. We are at your service."

In the days that follow, Lieutenant Bayard becomes my savior. From him, I learn that the only way to procure food and water on board—horrible though they may be—is to be part of a mess, a group of six individuals who gather outside the steward's room every morning and wait for the ringing of the steward's bell. Only then is each mess called by number, with one member lining up to receive the group's ration, served out of a small window in the steward's room. Without this designation, a prisoner is left to starve.

Bayard reorganizes the groups to ensure that I count as part of his mess. Becoming part of it means that not only do I get my daily ration of rancid suet, biscuits filled with worms, and weevil-laden peas, but I get preferential treatment for water. If food is scarce on board the *Jersey*, water is even rarer. Brought aboard from a farm spring near Wallabout Bay, it is in such demand that extra soldiers are needed to guard the barrels containing it. A gallon a day for drinking, washing, and cooking is the maximum allotted, and even with Bayard's assistance, I can never get enough of the brackish liquid. Perhaps most important, Bayard and his men protect me from the prison guards who long to brutalize me. They nurse me back to health after the periodic beatings I receive to elicit information about my fellow spies, and they buffer me from the most onerous of prisoner tasks—manning the pumps to ensure that the ship stays afloat despite the constant influx of water, and cleaning the latrines.

Bayard and his men operate by their own code of honor, an allegiance that includes information. They share with me their biggest secret: By day, Elizabeth Burgin, a widow with three young children in occupied New York, gathers supplies from prisoners' families and attempts to bring them on board, delivering personal letters along with food and blankets. By night, she and a man named George Higday row a small boat alongside the *Jersey*, delivering updates about the war and, very occasionally, smuggling prisoners off it, a task made easier by the lack of records about the prisoners held here. This brave woman, a lifeline to those on board the prison ships, undertakes this dangerous work to strike out against the forces that killed her husband.

Through Mrs. Burgin's brave efforts, I learn that Robert has been acquiring large sums of money, borrowing from everyone he knows, in an effort to ransom me off this ship. But I learn something else from Mrs. Burgin, a fact that perhaps Robert has not yet discovered: the British will never set me free, no matter the enormity of the sum he assembles. If Benedict Arnold's rage hasn't sealed my fate on the *Jersey*, then General Washington's decision to hang Major André for treason certainly does. No British authority will ever allow me to leave this ship alive.

My poor Robert. It pains me to think of him tormenting himself for the circumstances that have befallen me. My capture wasn't his fault. I hadn't been as invisible as I'd believed myself to be at the many social occasions where I eavesdropped on the British soldiers and at home in the presence of Officer Randolph. But it seems that Robert had been invisible.

I pray that he soon realizes that my only hope of survival lies with the victory of the Continental Army, and that he directs his energy and fury toward that end. Only then might he free me—and our baby.

# CHAPTER 13

September 14, 1781
New York, New York

Only my pregnancy, apparent five months after I boarded the *Jersey*, merited me a private cell with a window. Even then, bribes to Loring and Bayard's threats to stage a riot were necessary to make the move happen before I actually gave birth. Since I moved into this closet-like chamber, I miss the company of my mess, those honorable men who kept me safe for those first long months, but the small circular porthole in my tiny room opens to allow me to feel the sun on my face and the wind in my hair. After days and weeks and months spent in rank captivity, largely below deck, I cannot imagine anything better. And neither can my baby, once little Robert arrives one terrifying night.

With his brown hair and matching eyes, so like his father's in coloring, he resembles Robert in his nature as well. Serious and curious—with deep, penetrating gazes—he is a lovely gift in this horrendous place, even with the challenges of feeding him and keeping him clean. We spend many happy days alone in that minuscule cell, with only a hammock in one corner and a bucket in the other. We have our window, and we have each other. As we enjoy the simple pleasures of the sun's warmth and the gentle spray of salt water from a rogue gust of wind—with the baby kicking gleefully—I only wish for my husband.

He is in hiding, his invisibility finally giving way. I hear the news through the men in my mess, who whisper the information they glean from Mrs. Burgin in the morning distribution of rations. I knew the British would eventually identify him once they found me and undertook their investigation.

Feeding the baby, who is healthy and robust despite our surroundings, drains the last vestiges of my energy each day. As he grows, I wane. Bayard and his men slip me extra food and water they can ill spare—the odd hard-boiled egg, an occasional half-rotten apple, even hard biscuits shaken free of the worms—and while the nourishment is welcome, I know I will only be able to sustain little Robert for so long. Pleas to Loring and his men to allow my baby to leave are met with derision and laughter; they'll grant his freedom only in exchange for the names of my fellow spies, I am told. And even then, I know they will never let me or my baby go.

But I have a plan, one forged with Bayard's guidance in the long, dark winter nights of my pregnancy. I began my preparations before I even left the hull, and I continue them now. Bit by bit, I tear strips of fabric from the many-layered petticoat under my lilac gown, knotting them into a makeshift rope. When it reaches the length that Bayard told me was necessary, I begin weaving a tiny hammock to attach to one end, all of which I keep hidden under my filthy skirt. And then I wait for the full moon, and the signal.

One September morning, Bayard whispers to me, "It is time," with a squeeze of my hand. He alone knows how terrible and wonderful tonight will be. As the sun recedes on the horizon and my tiny cell darkens, I sing lullabies to my baby, asleep on my breast. I listen to his soft breathing and feel the lift of his chest. I want to savor every last sensation while I can.

Then I hear it, the sound of the oar in the water. Keeping little Robert close, I rise and peer out the window, down into the vast, dark ocean. In the light emitted from the moon, I see the outline of the rowboat and the silhouettes of two figures waiting directly below my cell.

I hesitate, tears streaming down my face. How can I part from my baby? Will he be safe as I lower him into Mrs. Burgin's boat? But then I think, *How can I not give him an opportunity at life—a life with his father, no less—knowing his slim chances of survival on board the* Jersey?

Sobbing silently, I wrap my sleeping baby in the hammock I fashioned especially for him. I check the safety of its harness and the strength of the rope. Time is ticking away too fast, I know, and I must act with haste, but how can I say goodbye? *Quickly,* I think, *or not at all.* I kiss him one last time on his soft cheek, slide him through the porthole, and lower him down the side of the *Jersey.*

Praying that he will not cry and alert the guards, I watch as a figure stands up on the rowboat and reaches for him. *He is safe,* I think, as I watch the rowboat fade into the distance. And I am left with a crippling mix of relief and despair.

I slide down the wall and sit in a heap on the rough wooden floor. How will I survive the *Jersey* without him? His sweet smile, his solemn stare, his gentle breath. It is then that I realize, fully and completely for the first time, that I will not.

Reaching deep into my dress pocket, I slide out my wedding ring and think about the future reunion of both my darling Roberts, and this alone gives me peace. The image of my husband flashes through my mind and I smile, thinking on our stolen moments together, spent plotting the downfall of the British.

One particular conversation surfaces with special vividness, in which I lamented the invisibility of women, even when it assisted me in my work for the Culper Ring. *How I long for true invisibility now,* I think. With it, I would not need to rely on my work for the Revolution and on my child to liberate me from this hell by establishing a legacy for me after I am gone. Instead, I could pass specter-like through the walls of the *Jersey* directly into freedom—and only then, into history.

# AUTHOR'S NOTE

This story about Agent 355 grew out of my mission. What exactly is that mission? Well, through my novels, I am determined to excavate from the past the most important, complex, and fascinating women of history and bring their stories into the light of the present day, where we can finally perceive their contributions as well as the insights they bring to modern-day issues. While I was knee-deep in research about the Revolutionary War, considering some of the Founding *Mothers* as possible book subjects, I came across the dangerous espionage work undertaken by the mysterious female Agent 355. Once I understood the importance of her extraordinary efforts to the outcome of the Revolutionary War, I knew I had to turn my attention to her story.

Agent 355 first became known when letters surfaced from members of George Washington's famous New York–based Culper Spy Ring, in which Robert Townsend mentioned a lady of his acquaintance who was well-positioned to assist them in their efforts to gather information about the British. Using the Culper Ring's code, he referred to this woman as Agent 355. Given Townsend's residence in New York City and given that the intelligence he gathered in the months that followed came from someone with close access to British spymaster Major André and his men, historians have assumed that Agent 355 was a New Yorker, someone with social connections that would give her access to overheard conversations between André and his fellow officers. These were conversations that, of course, the British would not expect a *woman* to understand, including discussions about Major André's secret agreement with Gen. Benedict Arnold to betray the Continental Army and deliver West Point to the British.

Since the discovery of those letters, several historical women have been floated as possible candidates for the role of Agent 355—from various family members and friends of Townsend to Benedict Arnold's own wife, Peggy, to a young woman referred to as Betty Floyd, assumed to be related to William Floyd, a signer of the Declaration of Independence and a delegate in the Continental Congress. Upon close assessment, however, none of these contenders seemed to fit. While many were brave patriots who undertook heroic work on behalf of the Revolutionary War, those women could not have been Agent 355 because they either weren't in New York City at the time in question or did not have the necessary contact with Major André and his officers.

But when I took one of the names that kept cropping up as a possibility—Betty Floyd—and examined her and the surname Floyd through a slightly different lens, I thought I might have a prospect for the Agent 355 of my story. Many of the members of the Culper Spy Ring, in fact, were in some way connected with William Floyd and his kin, either as neighbors or family members, as is the case with Townsend, his fellow agent Abraham Woodhull, and the creator of the Culper Ring itself, Benjamin Tallmadge (who later became Floyd's son-in-law). What if Betty Floyd wasn't the specific relative of William Floyd that historians had presumed and ruled out, but a distant relation of the Floyd family with a different surname—someone who'd become known as Floyd over time, due to her connection to the patriotic family?

Only then did I realize that I had *my* Agent 355—a brave young woman with rebellious ideals living in New York City with her affluent, British-supporting parents amidst the social whirl focused on officers quartering with the city's wealthy inhabitants. This Betty "Floyd" would have had ready access to Major André and his men, as well as Robert Townsend through his work as a merchant shop owner or as a writer for the *Royal Gazette*, which gave him entree to social occasions. And this Betty "Floyd" could have ultimately been caught and imprisoned on the horrific HMS *Jersey*, an incarceration that would explain Robert Townsend's reportedly panicked flight from New York, his desperate scrounging for ransom money, and his raising a child named Robert Townsend, Jr., who, incidentally, was instrumental in constructing the Prison Ship Martyrs Monument (a memorial to the many American prisoners who died in the British prison ships during the course of the Revolutionary War) when he reached adulthood.

We will probably never know the identity of the real Agent 355, and it is likely that my fictional version is just that— fictional. But she existed, and whoever she truly was, we owe her a debt of gratitude as a nation. Her heroism and contributions deserve to be widely known. Without the skillful espionage we attribute to her, the duplicity of Benedict Arnold might not have been discovered in time, and the British might have taken hold of the strategic West Point. Who knows what impact that might have had in the outcome of the Revolutionary War? How much of our freedom is due to Agent 355's courage and sacrifice?

Clearly, Agent 355—whoever she might have been—should join the pantheon of historical figures we admire. But until we change the chronicle of the past to include women and their legacies, we will continue to view the past more restrictively than it was, and we risk carrying those perspectives over into the future, perpetuating the pervasive marginalization of women's contributions. Rewriting the historical narrative to include women from all eras—where they've been all along, working but hiding in plain sight—is my mission.

# ABOUT THE AUTHOR

Marie Benedict is a *New York Times*– and *USA Today*–bestselling author of historical fiction, including *The Mystery of Mrs. Christie*, *The Only Woman in the Room*, *Carnegie's Maid*, and *The Other Einstein*. With Victoria Christopher Murray, Benedict co-wrote the Good Morning America Book Club Pick and *New York Times* bestseller, *The Personal Librarian*, and *The First Ladies*, also a *New York Times* bestseller. Writing as Heather Terrell, she has also published the novels *The Chrysalis*, *The Map Thief*, and *Brigid of Kildare*. Benedict lives in Pittsburgh, Pennsylvania, with her family. She can be found at authormariebenedict.com

INTEGRATED MEDIA

Find a full list of our authors and
titles at www.openroadmedia.com

FOLLOW US
@OpenRoadMedia